I0749210

THE SHOP THAT SOLD TRUTH

TAHIR SHAH

THE SHOP THAT SOLD TRUTH

A Teaching Story

TAHIR SHAH

MMXXIV

Secretum Mundi Publishing Ltd
124 City Road
London
EC1V 2NX
United Kingdom

www.secretum-mundi.com
info@secretum-mundi.com

First published by Secretum Mundi Publishing Ltd, 2024
A version of this story originally appeared in *Scorpion Soup* by Tahir Shah, 2013

THE SHOP THAT SOLD TRUTH

A CIP catalogue record for this title is available from the British Library.

ISBN 978-1-915876-13-3

VERSION 17082023

Visit the author's website:
Tahirshah.com

A blind dog follows the scent most keenly.

Egyptian saying

Teaching Stories

When I was small, I was told stories from morning till night.

I was told stories about genies and witches and about great birds that could carry away elephants on their wings... and stories about distant kingdoms and magical lands ruled by warrior kings.

I was told stories of good and bad... stories of hope and others of despair.

I was even told stories about stories.

And all the while, I listened, amazed.

The more I listened, the more my mind worked... and the more I came to understand that these stories had a power about them, a secret lifeblood all of their own.

They were magical instruments, machineries that could alter states of mind and change the way we think.

But most importantly of all, stories can teach us, without us realizing that they are doing so at all.

Part of the default programming of man, stories are within us all.

Born into us, they make us who we are – they make us human.

Since earliest childhood, I have feasted on stories as a way of learning about the world, and learning about myself. They have been my dictionary and my encyclopaedia, my classroom, my guide, and my very best friend.

To descend down through the layers of stories is to be reborn, into a dominion of fantasy – one touched by real magic.

Pre-eminent within the great treasuries of tales, it is teaching stories like this one that have shown me the path to follow beyond the next horizon, and have made me the man I am.

Tahir Shah

Once upon a time in Upper Egypt,
there lived a farmer and his wife.

They had very little money, and every month they grew all the more impoverished until, one day, their landlord announced that he would evict them from the farm.

‘Tomorrow I am going to the town,’ he said, ‘where I will sell the last of our possessions so that we can have one good meal before we are thrown out.’

‘But what will we do after that?’ asked his wife.

'We'll throw ourselves into the hands of fate,'
the farmer replied.

And so the next day, he piled the kitchen table, the chairs, the bedstead and the pots and pans onto the cart and pulled them a handful of miles into the town.

By dusk, all the possessions were sold and the farmer had a pocket jingling with coins.

He was about to go to the market to buy some food to take home when he noticed a rather grand shop at one corner of the town square.

Not having seen it before, he approached it cautiously, pressing his face up to the window.

The walls inside were lined with tall glass jars. Each one had a label but was quite empty of contents. His curiosity piqued, the farmer dusted himself down and pushed open the door.

The unfilled jars were a little larger than they had appeared from the outside, their labels written neatly in gold script.

And it was the labels that
caught the farmer's eye.

Although he had left school well before his time, he had learned to read, and he read out the labels one by one:

'Wisdom, Hope, Perception, Deceit, Truth,
Goodwill, Remorse, Bravery, Melancholy…'
he frowned.

As he did so,
a hunchbacked salesman appeared.
‘Can I help you, sir?’
he enquired in an even tone.

The farmer jumped back.
'I noticed the jars through the window,'
he spluttered, 'and was so intrigued that
I simply had to come in.'

Dusting a hair from his shoulder,
the hunchback intoned:
'And what, may I ask, was it
that you found so intriguing?'

The farmer pointed to the empty jars.
'Those,' he said.

The salesman narrowed his eyes. '*And*...?' he hissed. 'What is so strange about them?'

'Well, er, how can you sell Wisdom, or Truth… or whatever?' he said. 'The jars are empty. It's as plain as day.'

Now growing impatient,
the hunchback cracked his knuckles.
'Whoever said that qualities had a colour
or a texture?' he asked angrily.

'But whoever said they could be bought and sold?' the farmer replied.

‘Who said they could not?’

The farmer blinked.
'I don't believe it.'

'Why not?'

'Because I fancy you're a trickster, who's set up shop to dupe God-fearing men like me.'

The hunchback stepped over
to the door and pushed it open.
'It was you who came in here uninvited,'
he said calmly.

The farmer was about to stride out
when something caused him to pause.

He slid the tip of his tongue over his upper lip.
'You think I can't afford your wares,'
he said. 'Well, I've got money.'
He pulled out a pocketful of coins.

‘So what is it you would like to buy?’
asked the salesman.

The farmer scanned an eye over the shelves.
'Well, it depends how much they cost,' he said.

‘They are all priced differently and sold in small jars of their own,’ the clerk replied. ‘The most expensive is Wisdom, and the least is Shyness.’

‘Why would anyone want Shyness?’
the farmer asked.

‘You would be surprised, sir.’

'Well, for a handful of coins, could I get a selection? You know, so I can test some of them out.'

The hunchback was about to refuse when he was overcome with a surge of goodwill. He glanced up at the Goodwill jar, fearing its stopper was loose.

‘Very well,’ he said, ‘after all, I am about to close for the night.’

The farmer soon found himself the owner of a sackcloth bag in which five small glass jars were jangling.

Just before he left the shop,
the salesman gave a caution:

‘Although they are magical,’ he said, ‘you have only purchased samples of my wares, and in this size the effect of each jar lasts only a single day.’

It was dark by the time the farmer returned home. His wife was standing outside the shack, and she was weeping.

'We can't go in,' she said. 'The landlord has thrown us out. I hope you made us enough money so that at least we can eat.'

Her husband pulled the sackcloth
bag out from behind his back.
'I bought something far better than food,'
he said.

His wife looked at him expectantly.
'I bought these little jars,' he said.

‘We need more than liquid, we need food!’
‘But they don’t contain liquid.’
The farmer’s eyes were wide.

'Then what's in them?' asked the woman, snatching one and holding it up to the moon.

'It's empty!' she scowled.
'They all are,' the farmer explained.
'And that's the point.'

The next thing he knew, a clenched fist had hit him between the eyes. His wife's fury knew no bounds. As he came to his senses, he thought of something.

Picking up the jar that his wife
had thrown on the ground, he uncorked it
and held the rim to his pursed lips.

He felt something strange enter his mouth,
something intangible and warm.

‘You’ve ruined us!’ snapped his wife
as she began to weep again.

Glumly, the farmer stood up.
'My dear, dear wife,' he replied, 'please forgive me. I can never find the words to apologize enough. You deserve a far better man than I, and so I will take leave of you and return only when I have made something of myself.'

'Good riddance to you!'
barked the woman.
But her husband had already gone.

On the ground where he had been standing was a glass jar. Squinting and holding it to the full moon as she had done before, she read the handwritten label – *Remorse.*

REMORSE

Within a day, the farmer had crossed the fields and reached the edge of the neighbouring town. He encountered a fisherman beside a stream, approached him and said:

‘Hello friend, do forgive me for disturbing
you. Oh, how very sorry I am. Truly,
I really mean it.’

Struck by the stranger's courtesy, the fisherman offered him some grilled fish for lunch. The two men became instant friends and, before he knew it, the farmer was invited to stay in the fisherman's home.

That night, he reflected on the day's events and how the course of his life had changed.

His mind wandering, he opened the bag and
pulled out the first jar he could find.

The label read: *Bravery*.

Hmmm, thought the farmer to himself.
I'd like to be brave.

Without giving it too much thought at all, he prised out the cork and sucked down the jar's contents.

That night, while the fisherman and his family slept, a band of thieves broke into the house, each one armed with a scimitar.

They came over the roof and in through the windows, moving in complete silence.

Then they sprang.

The fisherman and his family were roused from their beds, tied up, and relieved of all that they owned.

In the clamour of the attack, no one noticed the farmer sleeping in the kitchen beside the fire.

Hearing a commotion, he crept stealthily into the sleeping quarters armed with a cleaver. And hardly knowing how he did it, he took the attackers by surprise.

Within less time than it takes to tell,
he fought them all at once and disarmed
them all in a feat of unbridled bravery.

Minutes later, the band of thieves lay dead,
their bodies dismembered on the floor
of the fisherman's home.

News of the farmer's bravery spread.

The corpses were taken into the town's main square, where they were hung up for all to see.

A passer-by recognized them as the most feared bandits in the realm, with a handsome reward on their heads.

Before he knew it, the farmer was being received in the royal palace, where he was decorated by the king and rewarded with six bags of gold.

Hardly able to believe his luck, he bought an ornate carriage and fine clothes for himself.

Then he set off back to his village
to be reunited with his wife.

Unaccustomed to luxury of any kind, the farmer ordered the coach driver to pull up on the banks of a brook at dusk. He selected a spot beneath a sprawling neem tree, protected from the wind by an outcrop of rocks.

‘We will camp here for the night,’
he said, ‘and set off at dawn.’

The moon full above him,
the farmer found himself unable to sleep.

Eventually, his mind turned
to the jars he had left.

Opening his sackcloth bag, he removed the remaining containers and held them up to the moonlight.

But his water bottle had leaked some of its precious fluid and the writing on the labels had been smudged. As much as he squinted, he was unable to read a word.

‘I should open them all and release their contents into the air,’ he thought aloud, ‘after all, they could contain harmful elements.’

But something niggled at him and, before he could reason with himself, he had snatched one of the jars out, pulled away the stopper, and quaffed down its contents.

A few minutes passed and the farmer began to sense something. He could hear a distant sound, like the clatter of hooves galloping far away.

He looked to the right, then the left,
and realized that the sound was coming
from the base of the neem tree.

He leant down and cupped a hand to his ear.

A procession of ants was marching across a root exposed above the surface of the ground.

The farmer watched as they made their way
across a stretch of barren land beside the brook
and down a hole no wider than his thumb.

The bizarre thing was that he could hear them walking, and talking as well, and could understand exactly what they said.

He could hear the sound of fish, too, swimming through the nearby water, and a nest of magpies up in the highest branches of the tree.

But that was not all.

The farmer walked over to the coachman, who was asleep on the grass. Without quite knowing how, he knew the man had an eye condition that would very soon make him blind.

And he knew that the carriage he drove was stolen, the yellow lacquer having been painted over the red livery of the king.

With his heightened perception, the farmer felt truly alive for the first time. He thought of all the possibilities, all the things he could do with such a gift.

But then something caught his attention.

The ants.

He overheard one complaining to another:
'What a nuisance it is that we have to dig
this mineshaft,' said the first.

‘And that there are these huge yellow blocks of
metal hindering our way,’ said the other.
‘If only someone would move them for us,’
the first replied.

Wasting no time, the farmer started digging.

Within an hour he had unearthed forty bars of gold, the pure metal glinting in the moon's light.

'I'm rich!' he exclaimed. 'Richer than in my wildest dreams!'

The coachman was woken by the farmer's
outcry. Sitting, he rubbed his eyes…
and screamed.
'I'm blind! I can't see a thing!'

Loading the treasure into the carriage,
the farmer helped the old coachman aboard.
Then, fearing that the people of his own town
would recognize him as the impoverished
farmer that he was, he rode on and on
until he came to the next kingdom.

Once there, he rented a fine mansion,
found wealthy new friends, and set himself
up as a member of the landed gentry.

As the weeks slipped away and his funds were invested, the farmer became the wealthiest man in the land.

One morning, he remembered his wife.

In all the excitement of his new life he had quite forgotten about her or, rather, had suppressed all thoughts of her because he was having such a pleasurable time.

Changing back into less opulent clothing,
he set off in a simple cart to find her.

Some days later, he located her in the town near to where their farm had stood.

A few feet away from where she was squatting
with her hand outstretched was the shop
that had purveyed the glass jars so
many weeks before.

But the premises was abandoned, the windows smashed, the door hanging off its hinges.

‘Dear wife,’ said the farmer, approaching the huddled figure. ‘I have returned and, as I promised, I have made something of myself.’

The old woman glanced up, squinted,
and slipped back into the shade.
She was imagining things again.

‘It’s me, your husband!’ cried the farmer.

Within a week or two, the couple were installed in their mansion.

Days slipped by, and the farmer's wife grew increasingly used to the lavish lifestyle that instant wealth can bring. She spent a fortune on fine dresses, and was soon bossing her husband around as she had always done.

As for himself, the farmer spent more and more of his time in leisure until, one morning, he remembered the three remaining jars. He asked one of the servants where his old sackcloth bag had been kept.

It was brought to him on a golden salver,
rose petals sprinkled around the edges.
Opening the bag, the farmer
removed the jars.

The labels were far too smudged to read.
Do I dare? he wondered to himself.

There was the sound of his wife barking
him orders from the salon downstairs.

Grimacing, he summoned his courage, opened one of the jars, and quaffed down its contents.

As before, nothing happened at first.

The farmer's wife asked for a purse of gold, so that she might buy herself a jewel-encrusted necklace. Her husband opened his safe and was about to hand over the coins when he felt a shiver down his spine.

If I give her this money, he thought to himself, *she's going to ask for some more, and then even more, and very soon we'll be broke.*

So he put the money back in the safe and shook his head. His wife protested, but he walked through into another room, where he started thinking.

For the first time in his life, the farmer had clarity of thought, the kind he never imagined was possible.

He could think of solutions to
the most complex problems in science,
the arts, and in everyday life.

On a single day – the day on which *Wisdom* was effective – the farmer came up with solutions to a thousand things.

He worked out how to solve the kingdom's terrible water shortage, and where to mine the abundant deposits of gold.

He settled marital disputes and invented new machines, designed a new city from the ground up, and cured the king of the illness that was about to claim his life.

Before he knew it, the kingdom was wealthier than any other, and the farmer was celebrated as a visionary of the rarest kind.

Realizing his people no longer wished him to lead them, the king abdicated, naming the farmer as his successor.

A little time passed, and the new king's
initial celebrity quickly wore thin.

There were lines of people queuing around the palace, all waiting for an audience – for their king to provide a solution to their woes.

The farmer sent agents across the known world to find the shop clerk who had sold him the potions.

But each one came back empty-handed.

In a moment of desperation, he reached into the bag and fished out one of the last two jars. He had no idea what was in it, but felt sure it would give him the boost he so badly needed.

Unscrewing the stopper, he sucked down the invisible contents and prepared for what was to come.

An hour passed and the farmer's wife – now the queen – shuffled in. Angrily, she insisted on an increase in her allowance and demanded a new crown.

The farmer-king smiled tautly.
Then, clapping his hands, he ordered the
royal guards to take the queen to the tower.

'I've always despised you!' he exclaimed.
'And now never will I have to listen
to your moaning again!'

As the guards marched the queen away, the farmer-king called his household staff to attention.

‘I am doing away with you all!’ he cried. ‘I know that you have been stealing from me, and are spying on me, and I hate every one of you!’

After that, he sent a message to the neighbouring king declaring war, on the grounds that the next kingdom was using too much air.

Then he roamed the streets in his royal carriage as his soldiers arrested every third man and woman for plotting against him.

By the end of the night, the farmer-king
had been overthrown by his people –
all because he had drunk the jar
once labelled *Deceit*.

A new ruler was chosen hastily in
an effort to quell the disorder.

Stripped of his medals and dressed in rags, the farmer-king was taken to a small cell below the one in which his own wife was still imprisoned.

The cell door was slammed,
and the key turned in the lock.

The most wretched of all the cells, its walls
were masked in dried blood and filth.
'They'll hang you at sunrise,' said the
toothless jailer through the bars.

The farmer-king crouched down,
put his head in his hands, and wept.

'That's enough noise!' bawled the jailer. 'Any more and I'll come in and thrash you!'

Wiping away his tears, the prisoner coaxed himself to be strong. But his pitiful situation was too much to take.

The farmer was about to break down in tears
again when he remembered that around his
waist was a belt into which the last
glass jar had been sewn.

Taking a deep breath and squaring
his shoulders feebly, he said to himself,
*Well, what could be worse than what's promised
to me – a gallows at dawn*?

Unpicking the stitches, he opened the jar and drank down its contents.

A little time slipped away and the farmer found himself feeling relatively bullish. Indeed, given his disconsolate circumstances, he felt as though there was everything to live for.

Springing to his feet, he began making plans for the future, enthused about the little time he had left. The last grains of sand may have been running through the hourglass of his own existence, but he had quaffed a little jar of *Hope*.

At dawn, guards arrived to drag the prisoner to the gallows.

They were surprised that he went willingly,
walking to the place of execution with
a spring in his step.

'Do you want a blindfold?'
the executioner asked.
'No, no, no,' the farmer-king-turned-pauper
said brightly. 'No need. You see, I'm not
going to die today.'

The executioner balked.
'In all the years I have been hanging people like you,' he said, 'I've never met anyone so confident in the face of such certainty!'

As the prisoner had the noose fitted around
his neck, he broke into laughter, tears of
joy rolling down his cheeks.
'It's because I live in hope!' he exclaimed.

By chance, the new ruler was watching from a window above the courtyard where the gallows was positioned.

How can a man like that be sentenced to death – a man who behaves with such aplomb in the face of such fear?
he thought.

A whistle sounded and, at the last moment,
the execution was called off.

The noose was loosened.

Stepping down from the gallows, the prisoner was permitted to go free. He was even given a bag of silver with which to begin his life afresh.

That evening, having eaten well, the former farmer got chatting to a traveller in the teahouse.

'I have been a destitute farmer, an adventurer, a king, and very nearly a dead man,' he said. 'I have known remorse, bravery, wisdom, deceit, and even hope.'

The traveller shrugged.
'And after all your life adventures,
what did you learn?'

The farmer who had once been king smiled.
'To embrace the unexpected,' he said.

Finis

About the Author

Descended from a long line of storytellers, writers, and savants, Tahir Shah is one of the most prolific authors of his generation. He has published more than sixty books in numerous genres, including travel, fiction, and fantasy, as well as tales for children.

Raised in the tradition of Eastern 'teaching stories', Shah is passionate about stories and storytelling. He regards the ability to learn from folklore as being in us all, what he calls a 'default setting of humankind'. As well as having written scores of books, Shah has made documentaries for National Geographic TV and The History Channel. He is the founder and CEO of the charity, The Scheherazade Foundation.

Books By Tahir Shah

The Writer's Craft

The Reason to Write

Workbook: Comprehensive, Volume I & II

Workbook: Fantasy, Volume I & II

Workbook: Fiction, Volume I & II

Workbook: Historical Fiction, Volume I & II

Workbook: Teaching Stories, Volume I & II

Workbook: Travel, Volume I & II

Novels

Jinn Hunter: Book One – The Prism

Jinn Hunter: Book Two – The Jinnslayer

Jinn Hunter: Book Three – The Perplexity

Hannibal Fogg and the Supreme Secret of Man

Casablanca Blues

Eye Spy

Godman

Paris Syndrome

Timbuctoo

Midas

Zigzagzone

Nasrudin

Travels With Nasrudin

The Misadventures of the Mystifying Nasrudin

The Peregrinations of the Perplexing Nasrudin

The Voyages and Vicissitudes of Nasrudin

Nasrudin in the Land of Fools

Travel

Trail of Feathers
Travels With Myself
Beyond the Devil's Teeth
In Search of King Solomon's Mines
House of the Tiger King
In Arabian Nights
The Caliph's House
Sorcerer's Apprentice
Journey Through Namibia

Teaching Stories

The Arabian Nights Adventures
Scorpion Soup
Tales Told to a Melon
The Afghan Notebook
Daydreams of an Octopus & Other Stories
The Caravanserai Stories
Ghoul Brothers
Hourglass
Imaginist
Jinn's Treasure
Jinnlore
Mellified Man
Skeleton Island
Wellspring
When the Sun Forgot to Rise
Outrunning the Reaper
The Cap of Invisibility
On Backgammon Time
The Wondrous Seed

The Paradise Tree
Mouse House
The Hoopoe's Flight
The Old Wind
A Treasury of Tales
The Tale of Double Six
The Forgotten Game
King of the Jinns
The Destiny Ring
Changing the World
Cat, Mouse
Frogland
Mittle-Mittle
Capilongo
The Princess of Zilzilam
The Singing Serpents
The Tale of the Rusty Nail
The Unicorn's Tear
The Clockmaker Who Travelled Through Time
The Fish's Dream
The Man Whose Arms Grew Branches
The Most Foolish of Men
The Shop That Sold Truth
Qwerty
Renaissance
The Man With the Tiger's Head
The Kingdom of Blink
The Wisdom of Celestine
Dream Soup
The Skeleton Factory
An Unexpected Gift

The Problem Exchange
The Pharaoh Code
The Monkey Puzzle Club
Liquid Time
Cat Dog, Dog Cat
Princess Pickle's Laugh

Anthologies

The Anthologies: Africa
The Anthologies: Ceremony
The Anthologies: Childhood
The Anthologies: City
The Anthologies: Danger
The Anthologies: East
The Anthologies: Expedition
The Anthologies: Frontier
The Anthologies: Hinterland
The Anthologies: India
The Anthologies: Jinns
The Anthologies: Jungle
The Anthologies: Magic
The Anthologies: Morocco
The Anthologies: Nasrudin
The Anthologies: People
The Anthologies: Quest
The Anthologies: South
The Anthologies: Taboo
The Anthologies: Teaching Stories
The Clockmaker's Box
The Tahir Shah Fiction Reader
The Tahir Shah Travel Reader

Research

Cultural Research

The Middle East Bedside Book

Three Essays

Edited by

Congress With a Crocodile

A Son of a Son, Volume I

A Son of a Son, Volume II

Screenplays

Casablanca Blues: The Screenplay

Timbuctoo: The Screenplay

A REQUEST

If you enjoyed this book, please review it on your favourite online retailer or review website.

Reviews are an author's best friend.

To stay in touch with Tahir Shah, and to hear about his upcoming releases before anyone else, please sign up for his mailing list:

http://tahirshah.com/newsletter

And to follow him on social media, please go to any of the following links:

http://www.twitter.com/humanstew

@tahirshah999

http://www.facebook.com/TahirShahAuthor

http://www.youtube.com/user/tahirshah999

http://www.pinterest.com/tahirshah

https://www.goodreads.com/tahirshahauthor

http://www.tahirshah.com

www.ingramcontent.com/pod-product-compliance
Lightning Source LLC
Chambersburg PA
CBHW030520310726
48979CB00010B/1745/J

9781915876133